EGMONT

We bring stories to life

First published in Great Britain in 2008 by Dean,
an imprint of Egmont UK Limited
239 Kensington High Street, London W8 6SA

Thomas the Tank Engine & Friends™

CREATED BY BRITT ALLCROFT

Based on the Railway Series by the Reverend W Awdry
© 2008 Gullane (Thomas) LLC. A HIT Entertainment company.
Thomas the Tank Engine & Friends and Thomas & Friends are trademarks of Gullane (Thomas) Limited.
Thomas the Tank Engine & Friends and Design is Reg. U.S. Pat. & Tm. Off.

HiT entertainment

ISBN 978 0 6035 6323 2
1 3 5 7 9 10 8 6 4 2
Printed in Singapore

Duncan and the Faulty Whistles

The Thomas TV Series

DEAN

Peter Sam, the green Narrow Gauge Steam Engine, was a very proud engine. He loved to help people out.

It was early morning on the Island of Sodor and Peter Sam was on his way to deliver some trucks to Duncan.

Duncan had to go to Strawberry Grove with the trucks, and he had agreed to give a lift to the Headmaster and his new organ.

As they waited for Peter Sam to arrive, the Headmaster played a lively tune.

Peter Sam chuffed along as fast as he could to bring Duncan the trucks. He was in such a hurry that he did not notice a low branch hanging over the track. As he hit it, there was a loud crack. His whistle had broken off!

Luckily, the accident happened just near where Duncan was waiting.

"I can't go any further without my whistle," groaned Peter Sam when he reached him. "It would be too dangerous."

"An engine's not an engine without a whistle," said Duncan, smugly.

And just to prove it, he gave a big blast on his own whistle: "Paaarp!"

But Peter Sam said nothing.

Duncan chuffed away in a big huff. "Peter Sam is just jealous of my shiny whistle," he said, crossly.

As he steamed through the countryside, he whistled at some sheep. But they were so busy eating grass that they took no notice.

"Bah!" he fumed, even more angrily.

Soon Duncan came up to a level crossing where Elizabeth the Vintage Lorry was waiting with a farmer's prize bull. This time, Duncan whistled even louder and longer than before. "Paaaaaarp!"

"Stop that nonsense, Duncan!" said Elizabeth, sternly.

Duncan fumed furiously down the track.

"I'll show everyone how loud and important my whistle is," Duncan muttered to himself, as he chuffed along.

But Duncan had not noticed that his whistle had come loose.

Then Duncan saw Terence the Tractor ploughing a field.

"I'll make Terence take notice of my whistle," he said to himself.

"Paaaaaarp!" went Duncan's whistle. But Terence's engine was so loud that he did not hear it.

"PAAAAAAAARP!" went Duncan again. And his whistle shot up in the air like a mighty rocket, and disappeared out of sight!

"We can't go any further without a whistle," said Duncan's Driver. "It's too dangerous."

But the Headmaster had an idea. "We may not have a whistle," he said, "but we've got an organ."

For the rest of the day, Duncan did not make a sound. But the Headmaster's organ did!

It tooted away at every crossing and every stop, doing the job just as well as a whistle — although Duncan did not think so. He felt very embarrassed.

At last the trucks were delivered, and Duncan steamed quietly back to the junction, with the Headmaster's organ playing all the way.

"Look!" laughed Rusty. "It's Duncan the Musical Engine. Toot, toot!"

But Peter Sam, who had a shiny new whistle, felt sorry for Duncan. "You did really well to deliver your goods without a whistle," he said, kindly.

"Do you really think so?" asked Duncan, cheering up.

"Absolutely!" said Peter Sam. "Although an engine's not an engine without a whistle."

"Or an organ!" laughed the Headmaster.

And all the engines tooted. Except Duncan, who just smiled.